Pitara
Bundle of Emotions

Flairs and Glairs
Publication House

"Pitara- Bundle of Emotions"

ISBN No: " 9789391302337"
1st Edition
Language – English and Hindi

Flairs and Glairs
Publication House
Regd. Under MSME Act.

Disclaimer

This is a work of fiction and solely represent the thoughts of the corresponding authors of the articles.
Our editors have tried their best to edit the content of all the authors and check the plagiarism.
All the write-ups in this book are unique and are only published in this book.
In case any plagiarism or error is found, only the author is responsible alone, and not the publisher or the Compilers.

Cover Designing and Book Formatting
Shubham Shah and Ishani Agarwal

Acknowledgement

Dear Almighty, thank you for blessing me with the power and zeal to be able to complete this Anthology.

Also, Thank You dear parents, for trusting in me, and letting me work whenever I wanted. My family is the one who supported me for what I am today.

When it comes to this, Anthology, I would like to start with Thanking the Co -Authors, without your help and support, I would have never been able to complete it.

Thank you all of you, for being there. Much Love to all of you. I am glad to see you all standing by me.

Co Author

Shubham Shah (Founder Flairs and Glairs)
Ishani Agarwal (Co-Founder Flairs and Glairs)
Shivangi Jaiswal (Compiler)

1. Shivani Priyanga
2. Pragya Verma
3. Sheetal Dwivedi
4. Padma Srivastava
5. Sahina Ghugha
6. Vaibhav Gupta
7. Gudiya Tiwari
8. Mohanapriya.K
9. Krishna Motwani
10. Sonal Tripathi Mishra
11. Nisha Kumari
12. Zainab Saboowala
13. Priyanka Varma
14. Kalamkaar
15. Pallavi Sharad Gijre
16. Anjali Kumari
17. Gautam
18. Ms. Ishrat Jahan Noormohammed Khan
19. Danish Ali
20. Mahwash Ali
21. Keerthana Suriya
22. Diksha Motwani
23. Sakshi Sharma

24. Rida E Haram Khan
25. Kavitha P
26. Archishman Satpathy
27. Ayushi Agrawal
28. Darshan Patel
29. Sakshi Shrivastava
30. Khushi Arora
31. Shaheen Ansari
32. Pooja Gautam
33. Kinjal Patel
34. Richa Saini
35. Hansika Sr
36. Kareena Verma
37. M.Harshini
38. Raj Jot
39. Grishma Ninave
40. Bhawna Mehta
41. M. Haseebunissa

Shubham Shah

(Founder- Flairs and Glairs)

Shubham Shah, an entrepreneur at "Flairs & Glairs" a brand with dynamics in events organizing and cultural educational pan INDIA, is a 26yrs old guy who recently has entered the digital platform of imprinting emotions. He has initiated with his own open mic platform to help budding poets and aspiring writers under his brand named as "Teekhe Zasbaaat"
He is a commerce graduate from the Bhagalpur City of Bihar.

He states Writing has impersonated him since childhood and he has now been writing for over a decade!

Cooking, on the other hand, is his passion! He also mentions, trying out new things just tickles him!

When asked sir, Why SPICY EMOTIONS?

He smiled and added, "agar jasbaat teekhe na ho toh wo jasbaat kahan" Spices are all that blends! So do his words!

As a chef, he presents to you his dish! Hot and freshly served! Taste it! Feel it! Enjoy it! You can also find his writing in the Book "Teekhe Zasbaaat" and 50+ Co -authored anthologies. With his passion to explore opportunities across Platforms, he is working with keen dev otion and We wish him all the very best for his future ventures.

He is Featured in the International Magazine DeMode for his upcoming solo novel.

He is Approved by Ne8x for its Lit Fest, and is a Golden Star Awards 2020 Winner.

He is a India Book of Records Holder for his Anthology Satrang, and has the Grandmaster title by Asia Book of Records, for the same.

He has also been featured in Prabhat Khabar, Dainik Jagran, and a lot of other Newspapers in Bihar for his achievements.

He has been a proud co-author to

India Book Of Records (Title- Black)

World Book Of Records (Title -15 Wonders of Poetries)

India Book Of Records (Title - Aaina)

Vajra World Records Holder (Title - Gustakhi Maaf Hai)

High Range of Records Holder (Title - Gustakhi Maaf Hai)

Indian Book of Records

(Title - Road from Worst to Best)

Share your reviews on his

INSTAGRAM

@spicy_emotions
@shubham4shah

Or via email on

shubham2shah@gmail.com

To stay tuned to his work and opportunities follow his business Handles

INSTAGRAM   FACEBOOK   YOUTUBE

@flairsandglairs
@teekhezasbaaat

WEBSITE:

https://flairsandglairs.in/
https://flairsandglairs.com/

Ishani Agarwal

(Co-Founder - Flairs and Glairs)

Ishani Agarwal hails from the City of Joy, Kolkata.
She is the co -founder of her Community "Teekhe Zasbaaat"
and Flairs and Glairs Publication.
Been a Compiler for 45+ Anthologies, she is in the process for
more. Co-authored in 150+ Anthologies. She is a India Book
of Records Holder, a Vajra World Records Holder, a High
Range of Records Holder, an OMG Book of Records Holder,
a Bravo Record holder, a Forever Star Book of World Records
and an Indian Book of Records Holder.
Approved by Ne8x for its Lit Fest 2020, and Literary Icon
2020. Also a Golden Star Awards Winner 2020.
She has also been award ed with India Star Republic Award
2021, a part of She Awards by Awards Arc and Winner of Nari
Samman 2021 by Literoma.
She is also selected as Best Achiever of the Year by
AwardsArc and Most Challenging Compiler Award by
Spectrum Awards.

She got her first solo Published,a solo Compilation consisting of first 750 contents of hers, titled "Hand That Burnt While Healing".

She has been featured by the National Magazine "Taree Zameen Par" with the title 'unstoppable'.
Also featured in the International Magazine DeMode for her upcoming solo novel, she is proud to write on social issues, and is happy with the love she is receiving.
Connect with her on Instagram: @Ishani_agarwal_quotes / @compilations_so_far

Shivangi Jaiswal
(Compiler)

Shivangi Jaiswal is a Content Writer from Kolkata. Executive Head at "Flairs & Glairs" brand with dynamics in events organizing and cultural educational pan INDIA. Organizer at "The Glittering Fables" Writing Community. She is a B. Com Honors graduate. Certified in Stocks & Short Selling as well as Certified in Digital Marketing Been a keen student, she has recently been Certified for learning Spanish Language.

She is an Indian Book of Record Holder.
Approved by Ne8x for its Lit Fest 2020 for the Author of the Year 2020 and the Real Hero's Title 2020. Also, a Warrior of Change Awardee 2021
She loves to bring smiles and happiness to many faces, so she is into Social service.
Traveler, Teacher, Meditator, Dancer, Singer, Instrument Player. She loves to play guitar and harmonium. Also been awarded in many events for winning many categories Been a Public Speaker she has taken part in many events and nailed it. Been a great Adviso r to many. She has also been crowned for winning Miss Great Podium 2020 Title in the category Modelling recently. Sports freak of Swimming and Badminton with a passion so strong. Since, past one year she has started her writing journey.
She writes so that many people can connect with their stories and get positive hopes. She thinks " Every story is unique so embrace yourself to the best". She is a writer by day and a reader by night. Been a Complier of 3 2+ Anthologies, and in process for more, also Co - authored 1 20+ anthologies. Shivangi is an old soul with young eyes, a vintage heart, and a beautiful mind."

You can follow her work:
Instagram
@the_knockingvibe
@house_of_compilations

Tears of Smile.

Today I have something to say,
but my emotions and thoughts are
scattered all the way.

Abandoned by the way.
Struggling to express myself.
I keep looking
I keep searching

I don't know why but I'm speechless.
A journey through the shadow
Depression heavy
Rooted inside
Breaking down I feel all alone

The reflection in the mirror
Is no longer free to see.
Bounded
Chained
Empty I'm torn apart stored in pain.
Wrapped in the blanket of thorns.
Coming in the tears of smile.

Helpless

Feeling my way through my heart
Completely in the wind, utterly in the rain.

A delightful pain.
The feeling untamed, that continue
to remain unexpressed.

I wonder if it's ever existed.
Through tears and smiles.
My unspoken words
My unspoken pain
My unspoken happiness
And my unspoken feelings

Running far away from me.
Wailing across the sight.
Some words simply refuse to flow of
my soul and mind.
As if words are vanishing
My vision is blurring
And my feeling to life?
Is no more.

Depressed at its best.
Making me black and white.
Stealing all the color of my soul
I'm finally helpless.

Threads of Love

I'm stuck.
Yes, I'm stuck with my sorrow

Silently unexpressed
Burning all alone.

No one can fix it.
Things don't even turn out according

Emotions Balancing
A voice, a pain sour at the top
Like bars between us.

Being boxed on the wall.
Realising that people on whom you can trust is rare.
Things pinching inside all the time.

Feelings are left unexpressed
Threads of love are left unwoven.

Shivani Priyanga

Shivani Priyanga
She is the girl who is holding her swords in her words and sweets in her poem.
She had worked as a co author in the number of anthologies and she had written about 300+ poems in Tamil and English.
She is one of the emerging writers from Tamil Nadu who is being active on Instagram and yourquote as shivani_priyanga_quotes and Shivani Priyanga respectively.
Mail: shivanipriyanga@gmail.com

Her Fantasy

The frozen garden along with the melted fruits!
Just like the girl who is in love!
She never shares her secrets!
She admires the person,
But never express!
She desires everything,
Yet Fears!
She dreams nothing,
Inspite holds confidence!
For the future,
She sketches the beautifull story!
In the thought of him,
She forgets everything!
Her romance is not yet revealed,
The world expects the first look of her story'
Including her who haven't met her's...
She's the princess of her fantasy!
She's the queen of her dream kingdom!
She's the ruler of her unknown wisdom!
She's the thief of her mysterious mines!
Looking for his look,
She lost her way in his path!
He smiles in her eyes,
Made her day completely hypnotized!
She imagines,
He never knew her!
Here, she's thinking him;
Whereas
There, he's doing her things unknowingly!
The distance matters...
But knowing matters, right?
For the following life,
She carries questions
He carries her answers!

And finally,
In the exam hall,
In the part of match the following pairs correctly,
They won the first prize under fluck!
Either her luck or his luck,
They were made each other luckily!

Pragya Verma

Pragya Verma hails from Prayagraj, Uttar Pradesh. She is a poetess and a writer. She has done 80+ anthologies, and two international anthologies and currently doing two world record anthologies as a co -author. She is also compiling two anthologies named, " Shades of Night", "In A Relationship with Success". She has a great interest in making paintings and doing photography. She loves to gain spiritual knowledge and tries to find peace everywhere. You can follow her on Instagram: @wordsofpragya

Unexpressed Love

Childhood crush turned into love,
He was always what I was thinking of.
Watching him rolling up his sleeve,
My eyes weren't allowing me to leave.

He was the reason why I went to school,
Best part is to see him through windows.
Eagerly waiting for the breaks,
To just see his expression that he makes.

My girls used to get bored hearing about him,
Didn't know how to stop thinking about him.
Watching his pictures, stalking his account,
That was what my life is all about.

The time passes so fast,
All I had was one last chance,
But I didn't have the courage to tell him,
And now, all I have is memories of him.

My hidden love hasn't faded yet,
Now all I have is lots of regrets.

Sheetal Dwivedi

जज़्बातों को बयां नही कर पाती जब कभी लिख देती हूं इन्हें किस्से ओर कहानियों में".

Hey, Sheetal Dwivedi is an writer who likes to write her feelings in her unique sort of way. She participated in the various anthologies as a coauthor as well as she performed in the various open mic events. She likes to cook and singing is her hobby. She is dreamer and achiever and she believes she deserves to be successful and she is best in her own way.

<u>आखिरी बारिश</u>

मुलाकत की वो आखिरी बारिश याद है क्या?
आज भी तुन्हें वो अंधेरी रात उस रात की सिसकिया वो दोनों हाथो
का बिछड़ना याद है क्या ?
या रोजमर्रा की ज़िंदगी से उन पलों को निकाल फेका तुमने,
जो कभी साथ बिताए थे हमने,
वो बारिश की पहली बूद हमारी जिंदगी की आखिरी बारिश कि याद
दिलाती तो होगी ना जो हमारे जिंदगी में आई थी,
आज भी उन साथ बिताए पलो को महसूस किया होगा ना तुमने या
कहु की एक हादसे की तरह भूल गए हो उन साथ बिताए पलो को
ख़ैर मैं ये बातें किससे कर रही हु खुद से या तुमसे
तुम जो मेरे होकर भी मेरे न थे उस बारिश की बूँद की तरह जो सब
पर पड़ती है किसी एक पर नही
कभी फुर्सत मिले जो तुम्हे उन पलों को ना सही उस आखिरी
बारिश को याद कर के महसूस करना शायद तुम जान पाओ एक
बूँद की कीमत ।

कहा जाएगे इतने खुबिया लेकर,
कुछ खामिया भी रहने दो,
आखिर अंत मे ख़ाक ही होना हैं सबको

दिल-ए-नादान की आदतों को बदल लिया था हमने,
महज़ उनके कहने पे उसी राह पे चल दिए बिन सवाल किए एक
दफा फ़िर

जितना टूट कर तुम्हें चाहा अब लगता,
नहीं किसी को चाह पाऊंगी तुम्हारे शिवा

एक पल के लिए तुम सच्चे लगते हो और दूसरे पल ना जाने क्यो तुम
में से झूठ की बू नजर आति हैं,
बताओ ना कि तुम कैसे हो?
सच्चे?
झुठे?
ख़ैर जाने दो छोड़ो. ।

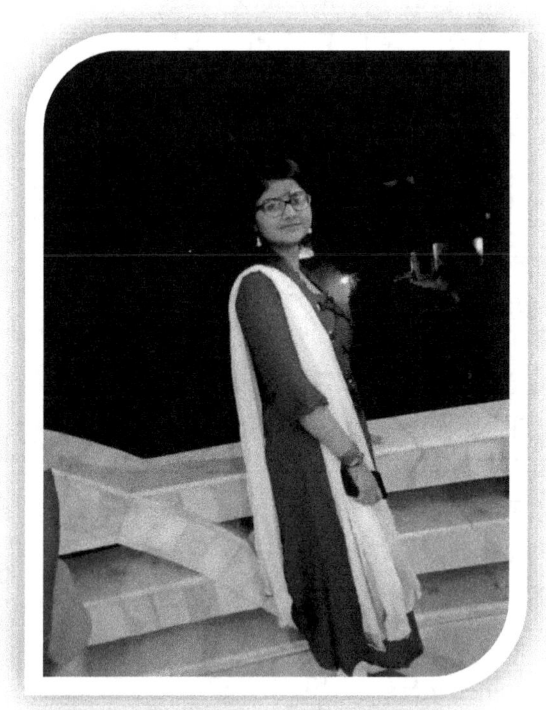

She is Padma Srivastava born and brought up in Varanasi and started writing from the age of 13year. She is a student of Archaeology with it she is also a good writer and singer. She is a nature lover but she writes all types of poetry specially based on bravery and philosophy. Before it she has been coauthor of several anthologies more than 10.

पिटाराः इश्क़ का

दबा रखा है एक गहरा पिटारा कहीं गहराई में दिल के

कभी फुरसत में मिलना तुम्हें दिखाऊंगी जरूर

कहते थे न तुम बहुत आसान है जीना अकेले

कभी तुम रहो उस मोड़ पर खड़े ना, तो मैं वो चाहे

कोई भी राह क्यूँ ना हो, तुमसे मिलने आऊंगी जरूर

कैसा होता है अहसास अकेलेपन से गुज़रने का,

कैसे बीतते हैं दिन अरसे जैसे ये

 तुम्हें अहसास दिलाऊंगी जरुर

सबके होते हुए भी अकेलापन कहते किसे हैं

ये भी तुम्हें बताऊंगी जरूर

कभी मिलो तो ज़िन्दगी के किसी चौराहे पर

आगे बढ़ना वाकई होता है क्या

 इससे रू-ब-रू कराऊंगी ज़रुर

सारी बातें तो झूठी ही निकली, वैसे निकलती भी कैसे न

इंसान झूठा हो तो भला बातें सच्ची कैसे हो सकती हैं

ख़ैर जो भी हो कहा तो तुम्हीं करते थे न

जी लेंगे सुकून से ज़रा आगे तो बढ़ो

देखो ना आज सदियों पुराने घाव भी दफ़न हैं

मेरी यादों में, कभी अगर किसी मोड़ पर मिले ना

हर एक घाव की मरहम भी दिखाऊंगी ज़रुर

अबकि तुम्हारी बनाई कहानी सुनूँ या ना सुनूँ

पर अपने भावनाओं का सदियों से बंद पिटारा

एक दफ़ा ही सही पर तुम्हें खोलकर दिखाऊंगी जरूर।।

Sahina Ghugha

Sahina Ghugha is 20-year-old b.com student at Saurashtra university Rajkot. She is from Jamnagar city of Gujarat. She is state level winner in poetry competition 2017. She is Co - author of 10+ anthologies. She is an amazing writer and poet and she wants do something for society through her pen.
Insta ID: -
Itz_Sahina_write

इश्क़ की हद

मेरे इश्क़ की हद से वो अभी तक वाक़िफ नहीं
बयां नहीं करते, मतलब ये नहीं कि आशिक़ नहीं

होती है महोब्बते छुपते छुपाते भी एक दूजे से
नज़रे लड़ती ऐसे शमशिर इनसे भी कातिल नहीं

हा है हम छुपे रुस्तम, जो अपने जज़्बात समझते
गर खुल गया राज़- ए- दरिया, इसका साहिल नहीं

है कुछ अनछुए लम्हें, जो छूने एकदुजे को दौड़ते है जो हद है हमारे
बीच, अभी उसे तोड़ने काबिल नहीं

बेहद पसंद है हमको, अपने इश्क़ को हद में रखना
बेगुनाह अच्छे है, गुनाह- ए- इश्क़ में शामिल नहीं

Vaibhav Gupta

This is Vaibhav Gupta belonging to Kanpur, UP. He is a graduate and had worked in hospitality Field. He has keen interest in poetries and stories. He has recently authored the e-novel "it happened in   Delhi" and is working on few more. Besides, He has been   actively participating on events those lead him to his passion. His works can be witnessed by his insta id- @thevaibhav_gupta

(1)

कहानी शुरू हुई हमारे सालों पहले ,
दास्तान अभी अधूरी है।
कुछ बातें कहनी जरूरी है,
 कुछ बातें सुनना जरूरी है।

मोहब्बत का मुकाम कुछ ऐसा तो ना होगा,
दर्द मेरा होगा तो इनाम तेरा ना होगा,
यूं ही नहीं बन जाते राहों में अपने,
तुझसे मिलने की दुआ कोई ,
मुझसे बढ़कर किया ना होगा।

साथ तेरा जो पाया मैंने,
भूल गया मैं दुनिया।
एक तेरी ही खबर रही मुझको,
जग की मैं ना सुनिया।

तेरे होठों की हंसी अक्सर करती बेकरार मुझे,
जी करता करो से बढ़कर प्यार तुझे,
तू पास बैठे हैं तो सांस थम सी जाती है,
खो जाता हूं तेरी खयालो में,
 जब याद तेरी आती है।

अक्सर सोचा करता हूं कि मैंने क्या पाया है ,
दुनिया को छोड़ तूने मुझे अपनाया है।
दूर किया दुख के साए को,
खुशी की चादर बिछाई हैं,
तेरी आंखों में देखूं तो लगे,
तू सिर्फ मेरे लिए ही आई है।

लोग चांद ढूंढते अंबर में,
मैंने मेरा चांद तुझ में पाया है ।
तुझे देख कर जी मेरा ऐसा चाहे,
जैसे बरसों बाद कोई अपना वापस आया है।

है सलोनी शाम वह,
जब तुम मिलने आई हो,
लगता है मुझे ऐसा क्यों,
 जैसे मुझ में तुम समाई हो ।

Gudiya Tiwari

I'm Gudiya Tiwari, daughter of Mr. Umesh Kumar Tiwari and Mrs. Rinku Tiwari was brought up in Bihar. Currently,   I'm pursuing my secondary education from JNV East Champaran,Bihar. I'm a passionate writer who loves to pen down my emotions and nature and strive to make my parents proud.
Thank you

Aisi Khudgarji Mai Kar Nahi Sakti

Tere najaro ke didar ka trj,
Jo chhed jaye mujhe andar hi andar,
Ishq ho ya fareb padta nhi ab koi frk,
Na khwaahis hai tujhe pane ki,
Na tujhe khone ka koi gum;
Kadr khud nhi kisi ke jajbato ki,
Or kahte ho shekhi mai dikhati hu,
To suno janaab-
Sidhi pahli ho ya aakhiri jindgi me,
Mai akele hi chadhna chahati hu,
Kisi ke sahaare ki jarurt nhi,
Kisi ki kamjori ban nhi sakti,
Khud ko kisi ke kabil kar lu,
Aisi khudgarji mai kar nhi skti;
Kahte ho ek dafaa Tere ishq pe aitbar kr lu,
Jamaane ka khauf chhod du,
Bs khamosh Tere dil ke alfaaj padh lu,
To gaur krna-
Dar iss nasmjh jahaan ka nhi,
Teri farebi muskan ka hai,
Yu hi badnaam h muhabat ki galiya,
Sara kusoor to kambhakht insan ka hai;
Aadat Teri dalkar jivan bhar
Uss Lt me tadapkar Mr nhi skti,
Teri ho jau isme koi harj nhi ,
Par dur hokar tujhse kisi aur ki
Jindgi fir mai ban nhi skti,
Khud ko kisi ke kabil kar lu,
Aisi khudgarji mai kar nhi skti.

Andhere Ka Sach

Andhera, jivan ka kadwa sach,
Kadam kadam ka hai wo sahchar,
Janm se hi Kali parchhai,
Apna kartvy nibhane daudi aai,
Kali koyal ke kook me hi,
Suraj bhi leta angadaai,
Ghani andheri raato me hi,
Chand ne bhi khyaati paai,
Nind ki talab me jab,
Aankho ne vishram kiya,
Andheri dariya ne hi usko
Swapn desh ka naav diya,
Kahi dard ka saathi kala,
To kahi aastha ki pahchan,
Kahi matam ka chola pahan
Hua hai ye badnaam,
Kali mitti me hi janm liya,
Fir q kale ka karte sb apmaan,
Mat bhulo, char kandho ke sahare,
Sab jate usi kale shamshan;
Ab tyag andhere ka mano,
Ya pap andhere ki maano,
Abhishap andhere ko maano,
Ya maano use mahaan,
Apani asatitv gwakar Jo roj,
Karta khushiyo se raushan sansar.

Mohanapriya.K

Co-author Mohanapriya.K is a good writer from Tamilnadu, India. She has completed her Bachelor's degree in Engineering stream. She has been a writer for one year as her passion. She wants to be a best compiler and   curator in future. Yet she sincerely hopes that this writing journey of her will bring her many successes. She also loves singing.

I'm Having So Many Emotions to Express

The desire to express his thoughts to others is obligatory for all of us.

But sometimes we want to express something but we don't get the right chance.

Others may not agree with what we say or they may not even be willing to listen to what we have to say.

One thing that can be more depressing than listening to what we say and not responding to it is the state of unwillingness to listen to what we are about to say.

It is right for a person to stand firm in his opinion and for that it is not right to refuse to even listen to what others are saying.

The desire to speak openly what is on the mind.

But sometimes unable to speak.

Because there are no opportunities to speak.

Opportunities are given or rejected by others.

Where we are coming from is not the fear th   at no one will accept.

It's like there's no one to listen to what we have to say.

His comments to him were correct.

In his opinion there is nothing wrong with them standing firm.

Unexpressed Emotions of Mine

Doing so may correct any mistakes in it.
But not expressing our opinions ourselves is not a betrayal of
ourselves!
There must be an opportunity for correction.
Because we have to bear the mental anguish that comes with
this betrayal.
We need to know who truly loves us and that is very good for
this stage.
Love can win,
love can only win love,
Times may change but the amount of past love we put on
someone will not change!
Never be afraid of retribution, sarcasm etc.
Do not be afraid to stop your trips to victory.
Because you know they are not true.
If so, why should you fear for them or why should you regret
thinking about it.
Everything that happens in this world depends on our hard
work and effort.
So, the beginning can be anyway.

Krishna Motwani

Krishna Motwani is a Student currently.

She uses to pen down her feelings.

She is a moody girl. She started writing in the month of june,2020. She writes in her free time.

She writes some motivational quotes or poetries too and practices artworks also. She lives her life like a bird   as bird flies freely and enjoys life like that she also lives her life freely and enjoy fullest.

For motivating and inspiring poems and quotes, you can check her on instagram : @ unique__blog_

दुख के पल!

कठिनाइयां आएंगी,
खुशियां दे जाएंगी।

बहुत कुछ सीखने को मिलेगा,
हमें लड़ना पड़ेगा।

जिंदगी की सबसे बड़ी जरूरत है हार,
हमें नहीं करना है अपने दुख का इज़हार।

मुश्किलें सिखा देती है बहुत कुछ हमें,
डरना नहीं है हमें उसका सामना करते समय।

हमें जिंदगी का हर पल जीना है खुशी से,
हार नहीं मानी कठिनाइयों से।

हर वक्त तो हम खुशी नहीं रह सकते,
पर यह हम किसी से कह नहीं सकते।

जिंदगी कभी लगाती है कांटो जैसी,
पर है तो वह गुलाब के फूल जैसी।

हर पड़ाव में हमें है हसना,
खुशियों को है कठिनाइयों से ही जीतना!

Sonal Tripathi Mishra

Sonal Tripathi Mishra, an MBA graduate from a renowned institute, a recruitment professional. Writing since a very young age, got published in different category anthologies, an avid book reader, music lover, traveler and an ardent fan of art & aesthetics. Loves exploring & working on different attributes of human emotions through reading, writing and painting. Trying to create awareness n love for reading in young talents in today's technology driven society through her book reading classes n activity sessions. A well-grounded individual who lives with passion, dedication and grace.
tripathisonal12@gmail.com
Instagram- alfaaz_sonal

पहचान

मोहब्बत तू मुझे मिलती तो है
पर क्यूँ तेरा चेहरा पहचानती नहीं
हाँ तफ़्सील से पढ़ने बैठूँ
तो कई चेहरे दिखाई देते हैं
तेरे एक चहरे में
पेशानी किसी और की
आँखें किसी और की नज़र आती हैं मुझे
वो एक तिरछी सी मुस्कान लबों की
वो नहीं मिलती बाकी नैन नक्शों से
और वो रुखसार पर पड़ा गहरा डिंपल,
साथ ही नाक पर ठहरा वो काला तिल
हाँ वही!!!
वो भी तो किसी और का है
सब अलग अलग जगह से
उठाये हुए टुकड़े हैं
क्या औरों के साथ भी ऐसा
होता है कहो
या कुछ अलग सा इश्क़ है
तुम्हें मुझसे
जो मिल जाते हो मुझे
अलग अलग किरदारों में
कैसे पहचानूँ तुम्हें
इन टुकड़ो में
बोलो कैसे करूँ
मैं तुम्हें मुकम्मल.

हरसिंगार

उसने कहा था
हरसिंगार के पेड़ के तले, मिलेगी मुझे
वो जब सूरज सिंदूरी रंग में डूबता होगा
और चांद उससे छुपता हुआ,
अपनी चांदनी बिखेरने के इंतजार में होगा
वो.जब चिड़िया अपने घरोंदों की तरफ
उड़ जाएंगी और
झींगुरों की झनझनाहट कानों में गूंजेगी
वो जब दिन का शोर, सन्नाटों की तरफ रुख करेगा
और खामोशी पसरने लगेगी...
सालों हो गये,
आज भी हरसिंगार के फूल वैसे ही महकने लगते हैं
शाम होते ही.
आया था मैं, जाने कितने ही दिन
पर वो नहीं मिली
उसने कहा था.
पर शब्दों का एतबार कहाँ |

Nisha Kumari

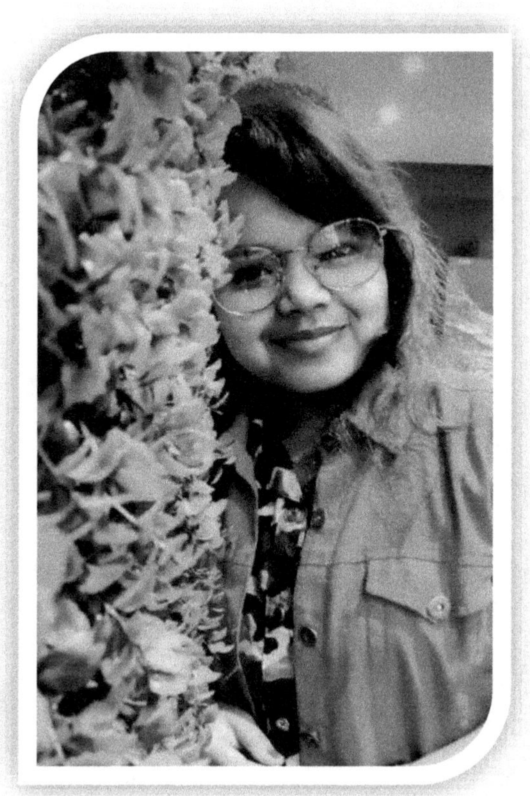

Nisha kumari (Nishika) is a student. She has completed diploma in civil engineering, now she is looking forward for further studies. She was born on 11th April of 1999. She belongs from Jharkhand, India. She loves to write fiction, nonfiction short stories and quotes. In her stories people can see different shades of life.

(1)

मुसाफ़िर नहीं हूँ
मुसाफ़िर बन आए
तेरी गली में.
बस एक दिदार को,
बैचेन मन को तसल्ली देकर!!

सूनी मिली वो गली भी
नहीं मिले तुम और ना मिला तेरा ऐहसास,
मंज़ूर नही सायद
मुकम्मल होना हमारा इश्क़ कुदरत को,
लौट जाना है अब मुझे अपना पता देकर!!

उम्मीद है अब भी
कभी तो तुम लौट कर आओगे
उस वक्त तुम्हें मेरे निशान मिलेंगे
तेरे दर पर!!

पुछ ही लिया लोगों ने
मुझे यूं बैचेन देखकर " मुसाफ़िर हो क्या? "
मुसाफ़िर नहीं मैं.
सालों साथ गुजारा है यहाँ,
किसी के अंदर.
लौट चले हम ये कहकर!

मिला था रास्ते में वो कैफे
जहाँ हर शाम तुम चाय पिया करते थे,
यहाँ की दीवारें, टैबल और चाय की प्याली
तुम्हारी मौजुदगी का प्रमाण बयां कर रही थी,
सब कुछ वैसा ही है
जैसा तुम जिक्र किया करते थे
लौट आई मैं एक कप चाय की किमत देकर!

Zainab Saboowala

Zainab Saboowala is a dreamer and believer from Mumbai, the city that never sleeps.

She's a night lover and works on being a good human rather than great one.

Her writings are her thoughts, emotions and feelings. She believes when you can't say it, write it.

All that makes sense is Pen & Dreams

Pen name - Zain

Instagram handle - @an. affectionate. Dreamer

क्या प्यार करना आसान है?

उलझी सी है ज़िंदगी
उलझा सा है ये मन
खामोशियों में दबी
आवाज़ें है बंध
सपनो के जरिए
ख्वाईशें भरती उडान है
टूटे हुए दिल से पूछो
क्या प्यार करना आसान है?
थामे हातों को
छूट जाने का डर है
उम्मीद भरी नजरों को
आसुओं का गम है
टूट जाते है सपने कई '
कोशिशें होती है बेकार
पूछो इस टूटे दिल को
क्या प्यार करना है आसान?

Ankahaa Izhaar

Yuhi hum tumhe durr se dhekte hai
Tumhari iss muskurahat pe marte hai
Tumhare kadam jaha padhte hai
Hum bas wahi chala karte hai
Din raat tumhare khyalon mein rehte hai
Hum tumhare deedar ko taraste hai
Palke jhapkane se bhi darte hai
Hum toh tumhare saaye pe bhi marte hai
Tumse itna pyaar jo karte hai.
Par dil ki baatein kehne se darte hai
Tumhe paane ki iss raah mein
Hum apni zindagi tumhare naam karte hai.

Priyanka Varma

She is Priyanka Varma studying   Masters of Pharmacy from Visakhapatnam. She is a National and Central Zonal Sports Player along with being a Classical Dancer and an Artist. Along with these, she is also a poetess fond of writing her thoughts. She believes that "Life Is A Bundle of Emotions and Experiences. You Must Be the Master of Your Emotions If You Wish to Live in Peace".

Humans the Bundle of Myriad Emotions

Emotion is the predominant and integral part of life.
Man is a social animal and man is a living organism as well.
Where there is li fe there will be emotions. It is the emotion
that has brought one man to another man together and formed
the society. It is emotion that differentiate us from non-living
organisms. Otherwise, we are lifeless and inactive body. The
man feels what other man suffers from. The best example of
human's emotions we can see from the mother fondling and
milking her baby.
Can anybody tell me why we start shedding our valuable tears
when someone dies in an accident?
Why our eyes flood into tears and become emotional when we
watch heart rending films?
Not merely mankind even all living organism have emotions
of their own. They laugh, they weep, they sympathize and they
boast.

Have we forgot emotions of Bharat towards Ram, Shabaree
towards Ram, Eklavya towards Dronacharya. They are all the
unique examples which is highly regarded in our life.
Emotion is the foundation brick of all human and his social
values.
If we don't have emotions, why do we start liking or hating
someone?
Why does the memory of departed or separate d sweet one's
haunt long after their exit from the worldly scene?
It is all due to emotional aspect of human life and immense
store of emotions in the core of our hearts. That's why we
lament, we cry, we smile, we over joy and we break if someone
or something hurts us.
Life is impossible without emotions. There are innumerable
emotions attached with human life. Love and hate are the part
of universal dualism. Either we love or hate. They are also

emotions. Love is god, love is life, and love is music and love are art as well. Nothing is above love according to the myths and modern thinkers. It is love that prompts a man to be friend of another man. That is first step of social structuralism. That knits the framework of society.

Desire, anger, sympathy, love, hate and friendliness are all the outburst of powerful emotions. Man is the most dominant, wise and powerful creature of the world.
So, to say man having no emotions is merely mockery of self as well as whole of mankind.
The man without emo tions is a stone, a lifeless object and everyone knows that lifeless object cannot make the world go ahead.
Without emotions we are robotic in nature that only knows how to perform the acts not why to perform the acts. This type of tendency brings catastrophe and large-scale destructions. Whenever human beings abandon emotions and gave much emphasis to individual ideas than communalideas, they had to suffer unfathomable loss like never before. The examples of dictators like Hitler, Mussolini and Napoleon are the burning and unique examples.

We Might Be the Master of Our Own Thoughts, Still We Are the Slaves of Our Emotions.

This is Kalamkaar. He is from Uttarakhand bought up in Meerut (Up). His hobbies are reading and writing. His interest is in writing. He loves writing. He is part of 350 +Anthologies as Co-Author. He won 300 + Certificate in Writing, He Start writing 29 February 2020. He is part of   4 anthology as Co Author going for record and He is omg record holder as Co - Author of Book Called Laposia. He is part of 6 international Anthologies as Co Author. He is simple and people observer. His insta handle is kalamkaar51 and email is kalamkaar51@gmail.com. He believes in Karma.

इंसान पशु के साथ दुर्र व्यवहार क्यों करें हैं

पशुओं को मानव हैं क्यों सताते
परेशान करने के लिए उनको अपने पास क्यों हैं बुलाते!
पूँछ मे उनकी बम अपने आनंद के लिए क्यों हैं लगाते
दुख उनको क्यों दे हैं जाते!
अपना एक खरोच सेहन नहीं कर सकते मगर पशुओं को क्यों चोट
हैं पहुँचते!
प्यार से इनको क्यों नहीं मानव रख पाते!
पत्थर मार कर बेजुबान को अपनी शान क्यों हैं दिखाते!
करने से पहले ख़ुद क्यों नहीं पानी पानी हो जाते!
दोस्ती उनसे क्यों नहीं कर जाते!
घर मे प्यार से उनको क्यों नहीं रख पाते!
बेजुबान जानवर को अपना स्नेह क्यों नहीं दिखाते!
घर मे रखकर उनको उनके साथ वक़्त क्यों नहीं बिताते!
परेशान करने उनको हमेशा क्यों हैं चले आते!
प्यार अपना पशुओं को क्यों नहीं हैं दिखाते!
साथ उनको क्यों नहीं रख पाते!
खर्चा शुरू होने पे क्यों सड़क मे हैं छोड़ जाते!
अपनी ज़िम्मेदारी क्यों नहीं समझ पाते!
दिल से लगाने के बजाये उनको अकेला और तन्हा क्यों हैं छोड़
जाते!

Pallavi Sharad Gijre

Pallavi Sharad Gijre is an engineering student from the rice city, Gondia (Maharashtra). She is a published writer. She has her best writings on love quotes, motivational and general topics. A bio is not enough to know about her writing, so give a try and read her write up.

Unkahi Baatein

Tumne kisi or se suna,
Par mujhse puchna jaruri nahi samjha,
Barso ki dosti ko parkha,
Aur mujhpar vishwas karna jaruri nahi samjha,
Duniya mere bare me jo bhi kahe mujhe parwah nahi,
Pr tumne maan kaise liya, kaise unko jawab karna jaruri nahi samjha,
Tumhare wo shabd sirf mujhe sunai dete hai,
Kisi or ne na suna or na sunna jaruri samjha,
Maine jo bhi kaha sabke samne kaha,
Tabhi toh meri baat sunna kisine jaruri nahi smjha,
Ijjat mangi nahi, hasil ki jati hai,
Jab tumne nahi kia to maine bhi karna jaruri nahi samjha,
Kuch galti meri thi or kuch tumhari,
Par ab aagey kisi ne baat karna jaruri nahi samjha,
Tumhare dost humesha se dhokebaaz the or rahege,
Mujhe unse dikkat nahi, par unke sath milke dusre ka majak na udana tumne jaruri nahi smjha,
Apni insecurities ko side me rakh dete, trust toh tha na mujhpe,
Fir bhi samjhota karna tumne jaruri nahi samjha,
Tumhe mere baat karne ke tarike se dikkat thi,
Mere character se toh nahi, fir bhi mujhe sahi sabit karna jaruri nahi samjha.
Tumhe mujhse pyaar tha yeh tumne sari duniya ko bata diya,
Par ek bar mujhe batana jaruri nahi samjha.

Anjali Kumari

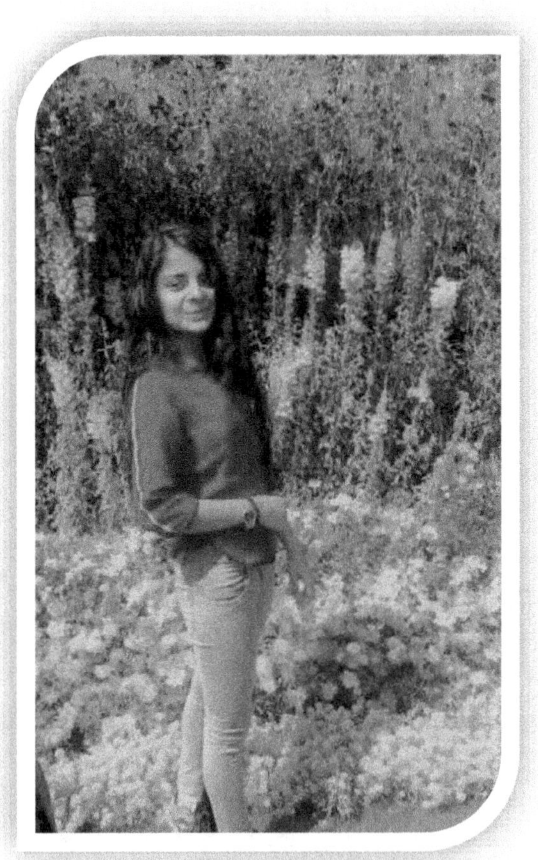

I Anjali Kumari from Delhi

याद

जो मुझे देता नहीं कुछ वो मुझसे मांगता क्या है?
समझ में नहीं आता ये जमाना मुझसे चाहता क्या है?

कुछ यू तेरा ख्याल मुझे आकर चला गया
जैसे किसी बच्चे को कोई बहला कर चला गया ।

बड़ा गुरूर था दरिया को अपनी गहराई का
कोई आकर निगाहों से उसे जलाकर चला गया ।

वो आया था ये कह कर की मेरी जीवन बिताएगा
बस पल भर वो लबो से लब मिलाकर चला गया ।

जाने कैसे कैसे ख्वाब देखती हूं
जब भी तेरे चेहरे की किताब देखती हूं ।

तेरा हरेक हर्फ रौशन करती है मुझे
मै तुझे देखती हूं या महताब देखती हूं।

कुछ ऐसा नशा है तेरी निगाहों में
लगता है जैसे शराब देखती हूं।

बरसातो में अश्क बहाना अच्छा लगता है
अब तेरी यादों को आना अच्छा लगता है।

तुझसे अब कोई तालुख तो नहीं रहा
पर राहों में तेरा मिल जाना अच्छा लगता है ।

अब तन्हा होती हूं तो कलम उठाती हूं
अश्कों से भी लब्ज बनाना अच्छा लगता है ।

खयाबो में अब भी तुम पहले जैसे ही हो
इसलिए रातो को जल्दी सो जाना अच्छा लगता है ।

जिन्दगी की सीढ़ियों पर एक ऐसा मुकाम भी है
अभी चढ़ते रहो आगे ढलान भी है ।

और यू तो शिकायते है उसे मेरे साथ रहने में
पर अंदर से उसे मेरे होने का गुमान भी है।

अपनी यादों को मेरा पता दिया था क्या?
मै रोई थी तो तुमने सुला दिया था क्या?

वो कहता है अब मेरी याद उसे आने लगी है
मुजको सच में भुला दिया था क्या?

पूरे घर में मेरे अल्फ़ाज़ गूंजते है
तुमने मेरा खत जला दिया था क्या?

Gautam

Gautam is from Karnal, Haryana.
He currently opts medicine as academics
and running Instagram page @the_writerdesk. He is a Gold
medalist in Science Olympiad and 2nd Runner up in   KOCA
(World's Biggest Youth fest). He is a co-author in many
anthologies. He believes that pen is always mightier than
sword. He loves to do writing, acting, vlogging, teaching,
singing. He writes because he felt that it is the   Bestway to
explore ourself and it makes him remind of halcyon days.

सूरज की तरह ढल बैठा हूं

क्या करे कुछ गलतियां मै भी कर बैठा था,
थोड़ा सा सचा इश्क़ उनसे कर बैठा था।

सोते जागते बस नाम ही उनका ज़ुबान पर रहता था,
लिख लेता था उनपर कुछ ना कुछ बस सुना ही नहीं पता था,
और हर बार दिल टूटने पर, लिखने का सिलसिला दोहराता था।

सुलझा सा इश्क अब उलझन लगने लग गया था,
जबसे हमें नजरअंदाज करना उनका अंदाज़ बन गया था।

चांद के भी तेवर बदल से गए थे,
अब वो भी हमें रात को बिना चांदनी के मिलने लगे थे।

उन्हें देखे हुए भी कई साल हो गए,
सुना है हमारे किस्से भी बवाल हो गए।

कभी कभी सोचता हूं ठीक ही था उनका दूर जाना,
जायज़ तो ये भी नहीं था, बात बात पर ख़ुद को बेइज्जत करवाना।

छोड़ चुका है जो तुम्हारे दिल के आशियाने को उसके आने का
कोई इरादा नहीं,
झूठा ना साबित किया हो उसने ऐसा कोई वादा नहीं।

हम उनकी ज़िंदगी में तो थे,
पर मुझ में उनकी जिंदगी नहीं।
मै मर रहा हूं रोज़ इस सच को बड़ी आसानी से झुठला बैठा हूं,
किसी शाम के सूरज की तरह फिरसे ढल बैठा हूं।

Ms. Ishrat Jahan Noormohammed Khan

Ms Ishrat jahan khan is a passionate Teacher and a Writer she loves reading and writing. Loving and caring is her hobby.
And keep learning and accept the positive suggestion is her quality.
She belongs to North India and stays at Ulhasnagar (Maharashtra).
Loves humanity always.

Hey Life

Hey life I miss you
I care for you
But never expressed to you
But always eyes were searching you

You can say it a passion
Or you can say compassion
Or feeling you my possession
And you were my emotions

You never hurt me
You never flirt me
Your never search me
You never perch me

It was you
It was me
It was heartbeat
And the eyes meet

Still life is searching
And always missing
Sometimes heart beating
And still, I am waiting...

Danish Ali

CA student. Nature lover. Poetry writer

(1)

आओ एकजहती के मौक़े पे ये वादा कर लें
देश में अपने फसादात ना होने देंगे
अब ना होगा यहां झगड़ा किसी मज़हब का कभी
अब ना रंगीन हम अखबार को होने देंगे

(2)

सोचा था उनसे मिलकर तकल्लुफ करेंगे हम
चाय का उसने पूछ लिया मना कर सके ना हम

(3)

अपने काजल को स्याही तुम बना लेती तो अच्छा था
मोहब्बत की नयी एक दास्तां लिखती तो अच्छा था
ज़मीन बेच कर शादी जो की है अपनी बेटी की
उसी पैसे से बेटी को पढ़ा देते तो अच्छा था

(4)

मैं उसकी हर दुआ पे आमीन कहता रहा
उसने मांगी तो किसी और से मिलने की दुआ

सच को सच तुम जो ये कहते हो गलत कहते हो
यानि इंसाफ़ की कहते हो गलत कहते हो

ये ज़मीं के नहीं, हैं आसमां से आए हुए
ये सियासत में हैं क्यों इनको गलत कहते हो

होते हैं ज़ुल्म तो होने दो और खामोश रहो
तुम जो आवाज़ उठाते हो गलत कहते हो

तुम को बख़्शा है मज़लूमों की जानें ली है
तुम मसीहा उसे कहते हो गलत कहते हो

(6)

जो भी मिलता था वह उसी का होता था
लहजे में इक ख़ास असर वो रखता था
कोई उसकी मैय्यत पे भी ना पहुंचा
पूरे शहर की हाल खबर वो रखता था

Mahwash Ali

Mahwash Ali is a graduate in Botany honours with distinction in chemistry. She did her schooling from Loreto and grads from Shri shikshayatan college. She has been one of the toppers of her school and college.

Contact her on- alizoya698@gmail.com

Bezubaan Ishq

Kuch Lafz ankahe reh jate hai
Jinhe samjha nahi pate hai,
Kehna toh bahot kuch chahte hai
Par bayaan nahi kar pate hai.

Wo samajh gaye hain sab
Is ummeed mein reh jate hai,
Kahi ankahi baaton ki
duvidha mein reh jate hai.

Zindagi mein kayi log aate hai
Kuch hasate hai
Toh kuch rulate hai,
Zindagi ki yahi reet hai
Jo hamein bahot kuch seekhate hai.

Tumse juda hona nahi chahte hai
Fir bhi bichad jate hai,
Is bezubaan ishq ki talaash mein
Tanha reh jate hai.

Keerthana Suriya

She is Ms.Keerthana Suriya a highly aspired, dynamic medical student, social-worker, a passionate writer and classical dancer who is engaging in self and social development, building relationships and exhibiting inte grity. She is Co -Author of various other anthologies.
She is Founder of WACHC Foundation - Women and Children Health Care and also holding the position of Women's Health Empowerment Project Head in the trust Women's Renaissance Centre. She strongly believe s that "When women and children rise, their communities and countries rise with them".
Follow her on Instagram - @keethusm

From Me - To Me

Dear Me,

I have found myself wondering
how many of these things?
I've actually never told you, and
things I really should have told you.
I know life has been tough for you
the past few years but you have
done quite a good job to stay alive
I know there were many moments of pain
but you got through all of it
You are a survivor

Thank you for staying confident
Thank you for the strength
Thank you for never giving up
Thank you for believing you are
important and you do matter.
Thank you for loving me even
when I was broken inside
Above all, thank you for trusting God,
for remaining hopeful despite all obstacles
Continue to be strong.

With love,
Me

Diksha Motwani

Diksha Motwani is a passionate girl from Mumbai, Maharashtra. She loves to pen her feelings. She is introvert but her pen makes her extrovert. She is a writer, singer, artist and a poet!

Can I?

I really don't know,
What this weird feeling is for,
I just want to hug you tight,
And cry out all what's inside,
Just want to have your shoulder,
To make me relief,
I just really don't know why am feeling lone and low,
Can you please be here for me?
Can I please cry?
Can I hug you?

Sakshi Sharma

Ms. Sakshi Sharma belongs Aligarh, U.P. She like to decorate her words and emotions on paper and has participated in various anthologies as co-author. She is biotechnologist and researcher by profession with more than 2 years of experience. Additionally, she is national kathak dancer. She wants to be unique! to stand out amongst the people and like to learn new things. She believes in delivering smiles on the faces.

अब कुछ बाकी नहीं

बहुत कुछ लिखना चाहती,
पर कुछ लिखने को अब बाकी नहीं,
सूखते हुए दरख्तों पे हरियाली की उम्मीद,
अब बाकी नहीं,
आब-ऐ-चश्म को यूंह हर दफा,
बहाना भी तो मुनासिब नहीं,
जैसे जिसे चाहा उसे,
ज़िन्दगी भर के लिए पाना भी मुनासिब नहीं,
अजीज़ हो जो दिल को, वो मिलता भी तो नहीं,
लिखना तो बहुत कुछ चाहती,
पर कुछ लिखने को अब बाकी नहीं....
एक पल में सजा सुना दी उन्होंने हमे हमारे प्यार की,
और हमें सजा कम करने की इजाज़त भी न दी,
और दिलकश बात तो ये है की,
हमें पता ही नहीं गुनाह क्या था हमारा,
उन्होंने हमें हमारी गलती बताने तक की माज़रत न की,
लिखना तो बहुत कुछ चाहती,
पर लिखने को कुछ अब बाकी नहीं...
अब कुछ बाकी नहीं...

अनकही बात

चलो बात करें, कुछ अनकही सी,
कुछ अलबेली सी, कुछ मस्त मगन सी...
कुछ खट्टी सी कुछ मीठी सी,
कुछ बात करें रूहानी परवाने सी...
कुछ तुम्हारी कुछ मेरी सी,
कुछ पीर सुनो दीवानी की,
कुछ सुनाओ अपनी कहानी सी...
चलो बात करें कुछ अनकही सी,
कुछ दिल की दुःखति दीवारों की,
कुछ अपने दिल के मैखानों की,
चलो बात करें कुछ भोली सी,
कुछ अपनी सी, कुछ तुम्हारी सी...
कुछ शमा के परवाने की, कुछ नशीली रात की...
जो दिल में रह गए, हलफनामों की,
कुछ दिल-ऐ-गुस्ताखी की, कुछ दिल-ऐ-दीदारों की,
चलो ना बात करें दिल की,
कुछ तुम्हारी कुछ मेरे दिल की,
चलो बात करें कुछ अनकही सी,
अनकहे जज़्बातों की, अनकहे हालातों की...

Rida E Haram Khan

Rida E Haram Khan is a seventeen-year-old weirdo with a touch of sass. She lives in Noida, Uttar Pradesh; and is currently in class 12, and would graduate in year 2021   . She has keen interest in English language and wishes to   study English literature professionally.

You can reach out to her on her Instagram-ridaeharamkhan or you may email her at ridaeharamkhan@gmail.com

Gone

I'll be gone,
With the wind
And a thousand memories
I will take away with me
All those hearts,
I have broken
I shall beg,
To forgive me
To end those feuds
I have started,
And shall seek mercy

Dark and bright, each shade of life,
We have come across
And all this time,
You held me tight
And guided me to the path
Which was right

I have screamed at you,
I have shouted at you
We had a million fights,
But I still love you

But before we realize it,
I'll be gone
With the wind
And I know you'll miss me too
And the beautiful friendship,
I had always cherished
Will come to an end too.

Kavitha P

Kavitha P is a woman with an   ambition and a heart of gold. Being a postgraduate in public administration, she has turned her cant's into cans. Inspired by her own name, she started her journey in literature writing in Tamil and English. She always wanted words. She loved them and grew   upon them. Words always gave her clarity and brought her reason. Hailing from the queen of hills, nature never fails to   inspire her. For her every word she writes is a reclaiming of wars she fought to be herself. She wants the world to know that each battle is worth fighting and these battles carve our self.

But I Want to Know

Words said are not pellucid but
Heart is flying with gossamer wings

The Moon, Lantern made for our dinner but
Here it's a day counter
Stars are flowers in my bouquet but
falling everyday

I'm tired of being mermaid and
I might die before you visit me...

I wish to turn myself as jellyfish, the immortal
I know, those transparent watery eyes will not
make you walk down memory lane

But
I want to know
Will you ever come to see me?

Archishman Satpathy

Archishman Satpathy, often called the Enthusiast Writer is a young dynamic writer from Deogarh, Odisha. He is presently pursuing B.Tech from IIIT Bhubaneswar. He started writing Quotes and Short Poetries from a young age of 16 and had now made it as his passion. He has contibuted as co-author in more than 50 anthologies. He is the author of the book " Lakeerein Zindagi Ke". Though he has a passion of writing quotes in any instance, he has also a deep love for Cricket.

Teen's Story

Always a teen is tested anyway
Is it a justice to the kiddos?
They are just started to live
They are just been a resource
And the wings of boredom
They got is the world itself
But still, they never complaint
Because they never knew that
The stuff they got is enough
We never tried to understand
The emotions of budding stars
That just not relax and enjoy all
What responsibility they get but
Is it really a justice that at any cost?
The lucky teens will be only tested.

(2)

Today I lost her battle of soul
I failed this time too in suppression
Whether I will care this battle or not
She will be alive forever in my genes
Let the favor work today at its best
Let her enjoy the depressed mine
I knew my version of this kind
Is really a painful and scared nature
But for my love I lost my happiness
I can't express the depressed mine
I can never expect such moment
When I have to write this to express
I promise that you will be remaining
In my core drops forever my jewel
With this I took a turn from my heart
Thanks for being with me for
Without you I can have never known
The importance of love in my life

Ayushi Agrawal

Ayushi Agrawal belongs to U.P. According to her, the pen is mightier than swords and words can bring a better change in the world.

she served as a co-author in 40+ Anthologies.

She writes her heart out and believes that words heal wounded hearts. She aspires to be a successful writer one day to reach millions of people with her writings.

You can find her writings on-

@wordsthatcanhealyourheart (Instagram) or reach her via mail ayushiagrawal1202@gmail.com

अनकहा प्यार

मेरे घर का वो मेरा प्यारा सा कोना,
मेरी छत का वो बरामदा,
जाड़े की वो सर्द धुंध सी सुबह,
बादलों के पीछे से झाँकता हुआ सूरज,
बिजली की तारों में झूलती हुई गौरैया,
हाथों में गर्म चाय का प्याला,
और मेरे सामने वो खिड़की,
खिड़की में बैठे तुम,
कैसे बयां करूँ वो तेरी अदा,
हाय! वो तेरी पहली नजर,
जब हुआ था मुझे तुझसे प्यार,
पर हिम्मत न कर पाई ये कहने की कभी,
की हो गया है तुझसे मुझे प्यार,
पर न जाने कैसे तू समझ गया मेरे वो एहसास,
और तूने कर दिया मुझसे
अपने प्यार का इजहार।।

अनकहे जज़्बात

कुछ बातें ऐसी होती है,
जिन्हें हम कह न पाते है,
रहते गुमसुम,
मन ही मन में दबते से जाते है,
कुछ अनकहे एहसास,
छुपकर हमारे सीने में,
भीतर ही भीतर हमें खोखला करते जाते है,
कह भी दिया गर तो,
मजाक न उड़ जाए कहीँ,
इस डर से भी छिपते जाते है,
हम ऐसे जज्बातों के तले,
खुद में ही सिमटे रह जाते है,
होकर भी भरी महफिलों में,
हम तन्हा से रह जाते है
हमारे ये छिपे हुए जज़्बात,
अनकहे से ही रह जाते है,
कोई समझ पाए शायद इन बेजुबान जज्बातों को,
पर हम किसी से नजरें भी तो मिला पाते नहीं,
कैसे कहे ये अनकहे जज्बात किसी से हम,
कुछ भी समझ पाते नहीं।।

Darshan Patel

Here by Darshan Patel physiotherapist, from Nadiad, Gujarat, coauthor who writes about life and with the aim to inspire a one and motivate to those who lose their hope in life and also about that fact of life. A true inspiration from chaanakya niti, bhagwat geeta, santram saurabh, social media, and learning lessons from one's life.

Bundle of Emotions

There were many emotions,
 that are going through out the life.
It can be happier, saddest, exciting, joyful,
as many from knife.
Stability Stagninity severity,
the way of flowing life.
The wondering with virtues of many,
come across me to live.
No wonder what happens to me,
for what it is to be.
Being in the boundaries of emotions,
that never affect the inner me.
The surrounding roller coaster,
moves in its way to live.
I knew what could be if over the emotions,
when the things went overwhelmed.
Therefore, to be in the stagnant flow of emotions,
is worthwhile required.
Then there could be ups and down,
Down to up, no matter what could it be.
It should be like coconut the hardest the outer,
And Softest the inner self.
So, whatever be the emotions should affect
Only the outer self not the inner self.
There are many attacks of hammer to hurt you.
But the real you won't be the mash the heart.
The life is full of colorful
Bundle of emotions that go through it.

Sakshi Shrivastava

साक्षी श्रीवास्तव रीवा मध्य प्रदेश की रहने वाली है, पेशे से ये DEd प्रथम वर्ष की छात्रा है, लिखना इनका शौक है, इनके लिखने का सफर अक्टूबर 2018 से शुरू हुआ, ये अक्सर हिंदी में कविताएं और शायरी लिखती है।

(1)

उसकी यादों को भुलाने में अब माहिर हो चुकी हूं
खुदा की कसम ना देना
अब एक काफ़िर हो चुकी हूं।

(2)

हम उनके लिए आंसू गिरते रहे जैसे हरश्रिंगार,
वो आंसू हमे ऐसे जलाते रहे जैसे अंगार,
पर अब नहीं रोना है बिल्कुल,
क्योंकि जस्बात आ चुके है अंत के कगार,

Khushi Arora

Khushi Arora is a student. Born and brought up in Delhi. She is a photographer, graphic designer, poet, writer, guitarist, and wants to be a psychologist in future. She loves to explore, trying her hands onto different feilds.she loves food, travelling and keen to learn new sports, languages and musical instruments. Growing up she started expressing her thoughts, opinions, experiences, imaginations and questions in her writings, which is more like a therapy to her. You can get to know more about Khushi Arora from her   Instagram account @starrry_eyed_dreamer

(1)

There is so much to say
So much that I feel
And if I start to talk
Would you ever believe
In the world wandering
Are so many souls
I need someone
To hear me whole
But in conversations
Will you hear between the lines?
Will you listen
When I'll be silent?
Will you feel
The pauses
The gaps I used in between
Each word
Exactly how I spelt it?
And then
Will you stay?
observing beauty in my mess
Which I know it is
But will you
make me believe
That I am not broken yet
That I am beautiful
And that beautiful is strong enough
To be broken again
Because you see
Words can act as medicines
To most of my wounds
Some visible in scars
Some hidden
I do not know
Where to find happiness

Will u share some?
I have lost mine!

Powerless to Escape

I have lost myself
In a storm of what if's,
In hovering over wishes and wants,
In balancing between like and love,
In people fading from life,
In cherishing memories,
In finding irrational possibilities,
In unrealistic realities,
In fantasized dreams,
In fictionalized imaginations,
In regrets of the past,
In Expectations of the next moment.
In figuring out my desires and needs,
In making non -existing choices,
In pleasing others
Often at the cost of my comfort
In filling voids,
In building bridges,
In understanding silences,
In fascination of happy endings,
Making sense out of meaningless pauses.
Now powerless to escape
The prison of my mind

Shaheen Ansari

She is pursuing Masters in Microbiology. And the one who try to put her thoughts in words of her imaginary world with her unique viewpoint. She is a free soul of a utopia with a perspective of protopia. Her viewpoint to see the world have always been come up as the hog heaven were everything is just perfect and fulfilled. To connect with her through e-mail shahiin.ansarii@gmail.com and also Instagram – shahin_ansari_22

Unexpressed Feelings

The state of mind deflects whether to say or not;
Some feelings which are unheard, unspoken.
Will it make things work or will destroys everything?
At time it gives butterflies in stomach and also fear of loss.
Don't want to suppress it and also wanted to be heard.
Sometimes try to keep mum and digest it;
Other times, just collect all the courage to speak up.
Will it be going to be said or will remain untold?
Will that make another person happy or sad?
Will I be depressed or be able to face the consequences?
Will I live with that unspoken feelings, my whole life?
Will I regret or just be contented for not saying it?
Will I always be in the misery of this unsaid feelings?
Or I just have to live with this whole dilemma?
Will it make my life easy or harder to live?
Will I going to express it or never be able to convey anyone?
Have I always been this confused person?
Or these unsaid feelings have made me one?
Will I be judged for expressing this feeling?
Or I will be accepted for what I feel?
Will it change the point of view for me?
Or will people see me from different perspective?
Will my feelings will be accepted or rejected?
Will that make any impact on anyone?
Or I will be the one who is common like everyone feel it?
Will I ever going to gather the courage to speak?
Or will it always be unheard and just vanish like other
feelings?

इनका नाम पूजा गौतम है। यह दिल्ली की रहने वाली है। इन्होंने इतिहास में स्नातकोत्तर और बी.एड किया है। यह ज़्यादातर औरतों की जागरूकता के विषय में लिखना ज़्यादा पसंद करती हैं या यूं कहिए ज्वलंत मुद्दों को उठाकर अपनी लेखनी द्वारा प्रश्नवाचक चिन्ह लगा देती हैं कि अन्याय और अत्याचारों का समाधान आखिर हैं कहां? इनको कविताएं, शायरी, ग़ज़ल, निबंध और लेख लिखने का शौक है और इन्होंने कई प्रशस्ति पत्र भी हासिल किए हैं इसी क्षेत्र में।

इश्क़ वो लज़ीज़ सा

इश्क वो लज़ीज़ सा, बंदिशों में खोया है
कुछ राह गुज़र ऐसे हैं, जो एक टक निगाह न देखें है
वो मुस्कुराहटों में बिखरा है, साया वो आफ़रीन के अक्स सा
वो मुझ में मुझसे जुड़ा नहीं, बस हवाओं में छू के उसे रहते हैं।।

ज़िन्दगी तू मुकम्मल नहीं

उदासियों के साये, अक्सर यूहीं बात करते हैं
ज़िन्दगी तू मुकम्मल नहीं, तजुर्बे बुजुर्गों के कहते हैं
मायूसियों में अड़ती है, ज़िद्द में अपने ही चलती है
क्या आश्रित जन तुझ पर है निर्भर, जो रह-रह मोहरे बदलती है।।

किंजल पटेल, आनंद गुजरात से है। एस. पी. युनिवर्सीटी, विध्यानगर से बी.कॉम और सोमनाथ युनिवर्सीटी से पीजीडीसीए किया है। अभी दस साल से हाइ-टेक कंम्प्युटर, बोरसद मे एक् रिसेप्शनिश्ट है और टैली एकाउंट पढ़ा रहीं है। इनका मानना है हर हाल में खुश रेहना क्योंकि जिंदगी दोबारा नहीं मिलती, वो बीते पल भी दोबारा नहीं मिलते। आपको जिंदगी मे कुछ मिले या ना मिले पर फिर भी कोशिश जारी रखनी चाहिए। क्या पता कहीं किसी मोड़ पर अपनी मंजील मिल जाये। लिखना इनका शौख है।

"मुझें पढ़ पाना हर किसी के लिये मुमकिन नहीं मैं वो किताब हुं जिसमे शब्दों की जगह जजबात लिखे है।

ना चाहते हुए भी तुझसे मोहब्बत हो गई

ना चाहते हुए भी तुझसे मोहब्बत हो गई,
ना जाने कब ये बेहद, बेइंतिहा हो गई।

तुम जो ऐसे बात करते हो,
तो अपनापन सा लगता है।

तुम जब ऐसे डांटते हो,
तब लगता है कोई तो है जिसे मेरी फ़िक्र है।

तुम जब ऐसे प्यार से समझाते हो,
तो लगता है कोई तो है जो मुझे संभाल सकता है।

ना चाहते हुए भी तुझसे मोहब्बत हो गई,
ना जाने कब ये बेहद, बेइंतिहा हो गई।

तुम जो मेरे आसपास होते हो,
तब वो हवाओं में कुछ जादू सा लगता है।

जब तु मुझे छुता है,
तब अजीब सा नशा हो जाता है।

जब तुम मुझे यूँ अपनी बाहों में समा लेते हो,
तब ये दुनिया, दुनिया नहीं जन्नत लगती हैं।

ना चाहते हुए भी तुझसे मोहब्बत हो गई,
ना जाने कब ये बेहद, बेइंतिहा हो गई।

एक पल बात ना हो तुमसे,
तो दिल मचलने लगता है।

एक बार दिदार ना हो तेरा,
तो दिल मे तुफान सा उठ जाता है।

तेरी आदत यूँ हो गई है इस दिल को,
की तेरे बिना एक पल भी शुकून से नहीं रह सकता।

में चाहती हूँ कि बता दू मेरे दिल की सारी बात तुझे,
पर ये दिल डरता कहीं खो ना दू इस जीवन मे तुझे।

ना चाहते हुए भी तुझसे मोहब्बत हो गई,
ना जाने कब ये बेहद, बेइंतिहा हो गई।

Richa Saini

Richar Saini..Richa is pursuing Fashion Designing. She start writing when she was 15 years old. She like to pen down her thoughts.Writing her thoughts gives a true happiness. She like to write deep feelings of herself.

इंतजार आज़ भी है

बददुआ क्या दु तुझे,
खुदा के आगे तेरे लिए दुआ निकलती आज़ भी है,

कहीं चले गए हों छोडकर या मै कहीं गुम हो गई,
पर तेरे आने का इंतजार आज़ भी है,

तुझे तेरी बातों को बेशक भूल जाऊँ मै,
पर मेरा तुझसे प्यार आज़ भी है,

सुना आज़ दोस्तों से की दुनिया कितनी खूबसूरत है,
पर मेरी दुनिया की खूबसूरती संग तेरे आज़ भी है,

बेशक रात खूबसूरत लगती है चांद सितारों से,
पर उन रातों मे मेरा ख्वाब तू आज़ भी है,

तुझे जिंदगी मानती रहीं हू,
कही तू मुझे पल ना समझे, ये़ डर आज़ भी है...

Hansika SR

Hansika SR is a Chartered Accountancystudent, also pursuing BCom (Acc/Fin) and a Carnatic singer by profession and a passionate writer, poet, a rhetoric public speaker and an enthusiastic learner of Vedic scriptures. She has brought numerous laurels through her versatility and her linguistic skills, is now a part of more   than 15 anthologies. She is a consistent blogger and quote writer on mirakee, yourquote and blogger.

The Forever Unexpressed!!

From being best friends, to realizing getting what you had for me,
I wished you expressed the unexpressed.

From making you wait longer, to wondering if you really stayed,
I cried watching you walk away, crumpling the unexpressed.

From patting myself at those little victories of trolling you, to being devasted of no contact,
I regretted why we left it as the unexpressed.

From getting used to a very new texting habit, to watching us not sustain it,
I broke myself leaving it again the unexpressed.

From being happy together miles away, to left every dream crushed,
Ego won the unexpressed.

From blushing the mutually unexpressed,
to regretting it all-over again,
We still chose to leave it unexpressed.

From thinking of retaining the special feeling, to forgetting to retain the bottom-line friendship,
We watched everything walk away as it was still unexpressed!!

Kareena Verma

She is kareena verma the Daughter of Mr.kehru verma and Mrs.Rajeshwari verma and She is a computer science student currently pursuing the Bachelor of Computer application , she has been writing since one year and a coauthor of many Anthology, A curious teenage girl filled with millions dreams of thoughtful brain ,In this world only her pen & diary is the best friend to penned her pain in the blank pages of life Diary .

And same as her name Kareena delineate alike her name, sanguine with her soul, pure with her heart, innocent with her straightforward thoughtful perceptions! For her Rectitude within her is everything & nothing is above than Viracity with our nation, she wants only to flame alike terracotta Diya, for one day she'll spread the happiness of lights as the   brightest star in the sky of someone home and just want to spread love of humanity everywhere!!

(1)

Dear Papa,

You never be known about my love for you ever, that's really true, the Communication distance make so
much distance between both of us,
I Can't able to express my feeling's
front of ever, you always think I'm very
Stubborn, egoistic girl, a silly girl who never be understand her responsibility always chatting with her friends and misusing her freedom, but today I want to tell you that
trust me papa!
I never become like that   girl, who will hurt you, I always fallow your valuable morality in my life, I always do Hardworking like you papa!
Trust me papa! One day sure I'll make you so much proud of you to myself!
I promise you, and maa - papa I can't live without you both ever!

My Mom

There are only two things you can't define ever with words,
Our mom and her love for us,
My mom so different from others mom,
I thought just,
 because see never be show her love to me,
Yes! But I feel every day,
When she scolds me for every small thing?
She is only the one my soulmate,
my shadow,
Who's know me better than Myself,
But sometimes I don't know,
Why she Always blame me for every mistake,
which I never he did to hurt her,
My mother's love always be unconditional to me, I knew
She sacrificed, she lost, she felt every unbearable pain for
me,
God made the most beautiful creature in this world is our
mom,
I just wanted to say you always,
Please believe me, I never be wanting to hurt you but
I just fell in love with you always,
just want to live with you forever
Just want to give you whole universe Happiness to you .

M.Harshini

She is M.Harshini .she is 23 years old .she is very well talented in writing poetry and a short story in both Tamil and English she has the talent to write poetry within 10 minutes after knowing the topic. She writes more and more in her Life.

# Unexpressed Love on My Soul

When I was a child,
I saw you in my life.
Before talking with you;
your smile has introduced me!
I have searched for you, who is laughing?

Something stops me to talk with you,
I do know what it is
A few days later, I slowly started
To talk with you
From my heartful words!

Slowly my mind falls in love with you!
I feel always happy; when I talk with you.
Until last, I never expressed my love.
with you in my life
Due to some reason.

Unexpressed Emotion on You

My dear Heart parts
when I saw you at first?
I was frozen totally
Because you are such a beautiful person.

I liked your love
Your affection for me
I liked your attitude
The situation you handled
I loved your companion.

One day You hurt me
But, because of my love for you
I am unable to express my emotions
And I controlled my emotions
And I express my smile on my face.

Raj jot is an ambitious poet and a content writer with a creative mind. He is a lyricist also. He thinks writing is the best way to express yourself. He belongs to Chandigarh. He is currently working as a chef. A multi-talented person. He is passionate about exploring the world. He loves to interact with new people and wants to fulfil his all dreams.
You can follow him on Instagram @rajjotofficial

वो एक लड़का है

वो लड़का है
कभी रोएगा नहीं पर सबको हंसाएगा
वो तुम्हे समझ लेगा पर अपने जज्बात नहीं बताएगा
वह लड़का है ।
तो घर की जिम्मेदारी भी संभाल लेगा
मुश्किलों से भी लड़ेगा
पर किसी को बताएगा नहीं
क्योंकि वह लड़का है ।
वह पढ़े गा लिखेगा
तो घर का नाम रोशन करेगा
वो सारे रिश्ते निभाएगा
पर कभी भी शिकवा जाहिर नहीं करेगा
और कभी रोएगा नहीं
क्योंकि वह एक लड़का है ।
धागों से अपने सपनों को बनाएगा
टूट भी गए तो अफसोस नहीं बताएगा
मशीन की तरह चलता जाएगा
सुबह से शाम तक सबके लिए सोचेगा
पर अपना हाल किसी को नहीं बताएगा
क्योंकि वह लड़का है ।
घर की जिम्मेदारियां संभाल लेगा
रोएगा नहीं पर सबको हंसाएगा
अपने आज को जिएगा
और अपने कल को भी सोचेगा
बीत गए जो पल उनको समेट के रखेगा
यादों को याद करके वह रोएगा नहीं
अपनों के लिए वह जिंदगी बिताएगा
वह लड़का है ।
वह रोएगा नहीं सबको हंसाएगा

हिचकियां

प्यार कुछ इस कदर है उनसे
इजहार है यह हिचकियां
खुश हूं मैं इस पल में क्योंकि यादें हैं हिचकियां
रात को आए हिचकियां सुबह भी आए हिचकियां
बरसात के मौसम की तरह है हिचकियां
कभी पत्तों पर गिरी हुई बूंदे है हिचकियां तो
कभी शाम को ढलता सूरज है हिचकियां
ईद का चांद है यह हिचकियां
तो कभी बनारस की घाट है यह हिचकियां
क्या नाम दूं मैं हिचकियां को
इस नमाजी को मिली इफ्तार में यह हिचकियां

Grishma Ninave

Grishma Ninave was born and brought up in the Orange City, Nagpur. She is a Science graduate and an avid reader. Thriller is her favorite genre. Currently working as a Project Head at Flairs & Glairs Publication House. A firm believer that happiness is not something tha t you find, it's something that you create. She loves travelling, blogging and listening to music.

क्यों आ गए हम इस मोड़ पर

क्यों आ गए हम इस मोड़ पर,
पिछले सारे रिश्तें तोड़ कर।

याद है आज भी जब तू पहली बार रोया था,
तुझे डर था कि तूने मुझे खोया था।

खुशी की लहर दौड़ जाती थी तेरी मुस्कान से,
पर आज भागती हूँ तेरी ही पहचान से।

इश्क़ होता तो रूठ जाती,
पर इबादत थी, ऐसे कैसे छूट जाती।

माना के साथी नहीं अब हम हैं,
पर दिल में आज भी तेरे न होने का ग़म है।

कोई आहट से लगता है कि तेरी परछाई है,
जो छुपके से मुझपे प्यार जताने आई है।

क्यों आ गए हम इस मोड़ पर,
पिछले सारे रिश्ते तोड़ कर।

Bhawna Mehta

Bhawna Mehta. She is presently pursuing B.Ed. from Guru Jambeshwar   University,   Hissar.She   belongs   to   town Bhuna,Fatehabad.She like to pen down her thoughts. She has written two blogs and she won one blog competition also. She has interest in other activities also. She also won District level Debate Competition and Dance Competition.

माँ

नौ महीने जिसने कौख में तुमको पाला,उसको जिंदगी भर तुम अपनें मकान में रहने देना।

जिसने अपना सब छोड़कर तुमको दे दिया,उसको तुम दो रोटी दे देना।

तुम्हारे लिए जो दुनियां से लड़ती रही,कभी तुम भी उसके लिए लड़ लेना।

जो खुद ना सो कर तुमको सुलाती रही,कभी तुम भी उसको सुला देना।

तुम्हारी सब ख्वाइशों को जिसने पूरा किया,कभी तुम भी उससे पूछ लेना।

वो कभी खुद से नहीं कहेगी,तुम्हे कुछ चाहिए 'माँ '।

यह कहकर उसको ख़ुश कर देना।

M. Haseebunissa

M. Haseebunissa is a young, aspiring and a vibrant leader
holding sound knowledge in theoretical and practical aspects
of counselling. She holds a Masters in Applied Psychology
and is currently pursuing her Master of Philosophy in
Counselling. She is a certified NLP Prac titioner. She loves to
write and believes in the magic of words to transform lives.
She finds solace in writing. Her work at various domains
involves promoting optimal mental health.

'Solivagant Soul'

For you my love
I would swim a million oceans,
But when I reach the shore, will I find you waiting for me?

Don't inflict pain in me, for you know I will love you still!

She was the moon he yearned for.
He searched for her in day light everyday
And gave up before the sunset.

7 billion people in the world and you my love, were the first
to teach me what pain felt like.

I am waiting for the kind of love where I wouldn't have to lose
myself to find someone. And I will wait, even if that takes a
lifetime.

When you said you loved me?
did you not mean my invisible wounds too?

It's all about who is willing to love you in dusk.

How you let others treat you says a lot about how much you
love and respect yourself

Flairs and Glairs, a platform by a student for the students. We are esteemed youth struggling to carve out our path for our future and we follow a basic mindset Since everyone is not born with allround skills. Joining hands with people who are born to execute it with perfection is the best way to evol ve. Self-Evolution is the need of the hour but, evolving as a community is what we strive for. The initiative as kickstarted by, Founder - Mr. Shubham Shah with the motive to utilize the skillset and talent of writing has now a team of 10+ people who are actively participating into newer forms of learning and discovering talents among youngsters. We Provide platform and services like Publishing opportunities, Open mics, Workshops, Hands-on training. Operating with Brand Name of Flairs and Glairs (Publication House), we offer the chance of elevating a passionate writer to an esteemed author With Brand name Teekhe Zasbaaat. We bring to you an opportunity to get accustomed with the Public Speaking and Presenting of Thoughts along with regular challen ges to brush up your inking spirit. The newest initiative to extend our services we introduced in a new writing Platform- The Glittering Fables and Ink Over Tears.

We Choose to Fly Like A Falcon than to be

a Leg Pulling Crab.

To Know More: Infoline – 7781900870
Mail Us At-
flairsandglairs@gmail.com / info@flairsandglairs.in
Or Visit is at
www.flairsandglairs.com / www.flairsandglairs.in
Social Handles- @flairsandglairs @teekhezasbaaat

www.ingramcontent.com/pod-product-compliance
Lightning Source LLC
LaVergne TN
LVHW050911200726

843508LV00011B/2177